Advance praise for

DIRTY WORK

"A little man with a huge heart and a huge
chip on his shoulder, Gulliver Dowd swaggers
into the crime fiction world and takes his
place with the great investigators. Smart,
vulnerable, wounded, heartbreakingly
hopeful, I just adore his company. This is a
staggering achievement. Bravo!"

—Louise Penny

DIRTY
WORK

REED FARREL COLEMAN

RAVEN BOOKS
an imprint of
ORCA BOOK PUBLISHERS

Coleman, Reed Farrel, 1956-
Dirty work / Reed Farrel Coleman.
(Rapid Reads)

Also issued in electronic format.
ISBN 978-1-4598-0206-3

I. Title. II. Series: Rapid reads
PS3553.O47443D57 2013   813'.54   C2012-907305-9

First published in the United States, 2013
Library of Congress Control Number: 2012952476

Summary: PI Gulliver Dowd searches for the daughter he didn't know
he had, who has gone missing under mysterious circumstances.

*Orca Book Publishers is dedicated to preserving the environment and has
printed this book on Forest Stewardship Council® certified paper.*

Orca Book Publishers gratefully acknowledges the support for
its publishing programs provided by the following agencies:
the Government of Canada through the Canada Book Fund and the
Canada Council for the Arts, and the Province of British Columbia
through the BC Arts Council and the Book Publishing Tax Credit.

Design by Teresa Bubela
Cover photography by iStockphoto.com

ORCA BOOK PUBLISHERS   ORCA BOOK PUBLISHERS
PO Box 5626, Stn. B   PO Box 468
Victoria, BC Canada   Custer, WA USA
V8R 6S4   98240-0468

www.orcabook.com
Printed and bound in Canada.

16 15 14 13 • 4 3 2 1

For Ellen W. Schare,
my favorite school librarian

CHAPTER ONE

The phone rang. Gulliver Dowd hurried to his desk as fast as his stubby, uneven legs would carry him. As he hobbled along, he shook his head. What good were cell phones if you didn't keep them in your pocket? He hated cell phones. In fact, he hated nearly everything these days. It seemed he had been angry ever since his sister Keisha had been murdered. Gulliver still recalled the old message on her phone.

Hi. I'm not home right now, but if you leave your name, number and a short message,

I'll get back to you. That is, if I survive my shift. Peace and love.

The first thing Gulliver had done after the funeral was erase that damn message. He had begged his sister to change it. He didn't approve of her tempting fate. He told her life was hard enough already. But that was her way. Keisha was tough, a fighter. Tell her she couldn't do something, and she would show you she could. That was half the reason she'd become a cop. People had said she would never make it. But her early life in foster care had taught her not to worry about fate. Problem is, things go wrong. It doesn't matter why, they just do. They go wrong for everybody sooner or later. Things had gone very wrong for Keisha. Deadly wrong.

One day she didn't make it back to the station house at the end of her shift. They found her empty patrol car on Pennsylvania Avenue in Brooklyn.

Its engine was still running. Her partner turned up at the Brookdale Hospital emergency room. He was barely conscious, his head bruised and bloodied. He couldn't remember what day it was or how he'd gotten to the hospital. He couldn't recall what had happened to him or where Keisha was. Two days later, they found her body behind an abandoned building on Livonia Avenue. Her hands were tied behind her. She had a bullet in the back of her head. The forensics report said she was on her knees when she died. Gulliver couldn't get that image out of his head. He hated thinking that she had died alone and afraid.

It had been six frustrating years. The NYPD had come up empty on Keisha's murder. He knew the cops had worked the case hard. When another cop is killed, they go all out. It didn't matter that Keisha was an African-American woman.

Or that she had only a few years on the job. Every cop knows the next person to get killed in the line of duty could be him. There were hundreds of clues to begin with. There are always lots when a reward is offered. But none of them worked out. The case went cold very quickly.

In a weird way Gulliver owed a debt to his sister's killer. He didn't like thinking that, but it was the truth. And Gulliver Dowd always faced the truth. No matter how ugly. No matter how hurtful. No matter what. When you looked like he did, you had to be honest with yourself.

Gulliver was so short that his reflection filled up only the bottom half of a mirror. That half showed him how cruel God was. Gulliver looked as if he had been built from mismatched body parts. His arms and legs were too small, even for his squat body. His hands were too big for his arms. His fingers, too small for his hands. His head, too big for his height. But the cruelest thing God had done was to give Gulliver a handsome face.

"What a waste," he'd heard a girl say during his first year in college. "What a waste."

Her friend agreed. "A pity."

Pity. The thing he hated most. If his face had been as ugly as the rest of him, people would have just turned away. People do that. They turn away from people in wheelchairs and autistic kids at the mall. They don't like being reminded of how much harder life could be. They don't want to know that in the next moment everything could be taken away from them. But people didn't turn away from Gulliver Dowd. Not at first. First they stared. Then they turned away. The looks on their faces said the same things those two girls had said back in college. *What a waste. What a pity.*

So Gulliver never turned away from the truth.

And if his sister hadn't been murdered, he wouldn't have become a private investigator. He wouldn't have gone from being someone who was always bullied to someone with a black belt in karate. For the first two years of karate his body ached. But he loved the training. His teachers didn't care about his looks. They cared only about results. If Keisha hadn't been murdered, he wouldn't have learned knife fighting from a retired Navy Seal. He wouldn't have learned to shoot or gotten a handgun carry permit. It was easier to become an astronaut than get a gun permit in New York. Gulliver did it by getting a job as a gem courier. It was dangerous work to carry jewels on the streets of New York City.

"Who is going to think anyone would trust me with diamonds and rubies?"

Gulliver asked when he applied for the job. "No thief is ever going to think, 'Hey, that little guy's carrying a few million worth of gems.'"

And Gulliver got the job. It paid well and suited his schedule. He still did some work for his old company when things were slow and he needed extra money.

Keisha's killer had taught Gulliver a lesson. If a brave, well-trained cop with a gun could be taken from her patrol car in daylight and shot dead, no one was safe. Gulliver meant to find the person who'd killed his sister. That's why he had gone through all the training. If the cops couldn't find the animal who had murdered his little sister, he would. He had pictured the murder in his head thousands of times. He started to picture it now, but the phone rang again.

CHAPTER TWO

H e waited for the caller to speak, but all he got was silence.

Tired of waiting, he finally said, "Gulliver Dowd Investigations."

"Is something wrong, Gullie? I can hear it in your voice," came the response. "What's the matter?"

Gullie. With both of his adoptive parents and Keisha gone, only one person still called him Gullie. His oldest friend. His only friend, Steven Mandel. Gulliver called him Rabbi. He couldn't remember when he'd started to call Steven that or why. Maybe because as a kid, Steven was wise and generous beyond his years.

"What's the matter?" Rabbi repeated.

Gulliver lied. "Nothing."

"Come on, Gullie, I know you for thirty years. It's Keisha, right? You were thinking of what happened to her." That was Rabbi. He had always been able to see into Gulliver's head and heart.

Gulliver confessed, "It was six years ago, Rabbi. And it still hurts like it was yesterday."

"I know it hurts. But maybe it's time to move on with your own life, Gullie. Stop looking for the killer. Keisha wouldn't want you to spend your whole life—"

"What are you calling about?" Gulliver cut him off. They had this talk about once a month. About how Gulliver should get on with his life. It never got very far.

He was never going to stop hunting for his sister's killer. Besides, what else was there? If it wasn't for the rage that drove him, he might have nothing.

"I've got a client who's interested in hiring you," Rabbi said.

"Who's the client? What's the job?"

"Since when did that matter to you?"

Gulliver agreed. "Good point."

"Meet me at Black and Blue Steaks at nine. Should be interesting."

"At least your client has a sense of humor," Gulliver said.

Rabbi was confused. "How's that?"

"Black and Blue is on Little West 12th Street. He even picked a street to match my size."

"Don't be an ass, Gullie."

"Can't help it. It's a God-given gift like the rest of me."

Rabbi hung up without another word.

* * *

The name of the restaurant, Black and Blue, was an inside joke. It referred to the way some people liked their steaks cooked— charred black outside, a juicy bluish-gray inside. But it also referred to the neighborhood. It had once been home to most of Manhattan's underground sex clubs. Many of them were for people who liked their sex rough or kinky. The clubs were still there. They were just a little deeper underground.

How did Gulliver know? It was his business to know. He never knew where he'd find a lead to his sister's killer. Besides, he was a finder by nature. Built with his nose low to the ground, like a hound. You would think his looks would work against him. The opposite was true. People dismissed him. He was often treated with amazing disrespect. Some people shouted at him as if he was deaf. Some people spelled in front of him, like he was a preschooler.

Some people spoke slowly, as if he was short on brains. He might be short, a bit malformed. But he was not deaf, not a child. He was also not stupid.

The thing that bugged him most was when clients asked, "What should I call you?"

"Gulliver," he'd answer, "or Mr. Dowd, if you'd like."

"No, I mean, no one calls you people midgets or dwarfs anymore. It's little people, right? So you're a little person."

"I am Gulliver Dowd, and if you call me anything else, you can take this job and shove it up your ass."

Gulliver had no time for labels. What did it matter what he was called? It wasn't going to change anything. He fell into a category of one: himself. He didn't want to be part of a group. Being in a group wasn't going to straighten out his body or gain him respect. He'd come into the world by himself. He lived by himself. He would probably die that way.

Gulliver got to the restaurant on time, and there was Rabbi, all six foot three of him. Gulliver came up behind him and gave his old friend a playful kick to the back of his left knee.

Rabbi acted like he didn't see Gulliver. "Did someone let their poodle off the leash?" he said.

"Screw you, Rabbi."

"You know, Gullie, most friends shake hands when they greet each other."

"Really? I'll have to try that sometime. Maybe I have a complex about my height." Gulliver hung his head in mock shame. "I'm too big to be a helper monkey and too small to be a jockey."

"That line is getting old, Gullie."

"I'll work on a new one."

"Let's eat." Rabbi turned to the hostess and said, "Reservation for Mandel, party of two."

The hostess was like many women in Lower Manhattan. She was thin, edgy and pretty in a pierced and tattooed way. She acted as if the world could show her nothing new. Then she spotted Gulliver, and her blue eyes suddenly sparkled. She looked at him as if he were a three-legged rescue puppy. Yeah, he got that a lot.

"No petting allowed," Gulliver snapped at her.

The sparkle went out of her blue eyes. "This way…gentlemen."

She walked them through the crowded main part of the steakhouse. It was all very modern and noisy. She led them to a smaller, more private dining room. In here the tables were far apart, the décor more old world. The tourists were in the main room. The real players sat in here. In the main room, the object was to see the beautiful people and be seen by them. In the smaller room, the objective was business, only business.

Steven Mandel was an entertainment lawyer. He wasn't a player, but many of his clients were. None were *hugely* famous, though many were quite rich. Some were soap opera actors or minor rock stars. Some of his writer clients were pretty famous and well to do. But today, being a famous writer was kind of like not being famous at all.

"So when do we meet my new employer?" Gulliver asked.

Rabbi said, "Steak now. Business later."

Gulliver read the menu. He smelled charred meat, sweet fried onions, earthy creamed spinach. But he also smelled trouble. Gulliver knew something was up when an expensive French wine was delivered to the table.

"We didn't order this," Gulliver said.

"Compliments of the house." The wine steward showed Gulliver the dusty label.

Gulliver nodded. The steward gave the bottle to the waiter. The waiter poured some into a bell-shaped glass. Gulliver liked cheap vodka much more than red wine. But that didn't mean he didn't like red wine at all. He also knew the difference between cheap red wine and the kind that cost hundreds of dollars a bottle. He pulled the glass closer. Sniffed it. Swirled it. Sipped it. Swished it and swallowed. He approved, nodding yes to the waiter. The waiter poured a full glass for Rabbi and then one for Gulliver.

"Gullie, you know your wine."

"The trick isn't knowing, Rabbi. It's looking like you know."

As they ate, Gulliver looked at his friend with wonder. Rabbi had been such a gangly kid. Now he was movie-star handsome. He looked like a young Kevin Kline with a more Jewish nose. Like a movie star, Rabbi attracted women the way a magnet attracts iron. It was too bad that the women he met were never right for him. In a way, Rabbi was more alone than Gulliver.

When they pushed their dinner plates away, the hostess returned. Gulliver realized she was quite good-looking in spite of the piercings and body ink. Rabbi also noticed.

"Gentlemen," she said, "would you please follow me to the Club Room for an after-dinner drink?"

They were led down a narrow hall. Then up a creaky staircase. At the top of the stairs they entered another world. Very old boys' club. Puffy leather sofas, wing chairs, green glass ashtrays. The walls were covered in walnut panels. Coats of arms and paintings of foxhunts hung on the walls. A bar was at one end of the room. The hostess stood behind the bar and asked the men what they would like to drink. Rabbi ordered a pricey tawny port. Gulliver ordered Chopin vodka. They sat at a vacant table.

When she arrived with their drinks, Rabbi reached for his wallet. She said, "That has already been seen to, Mr. Mandel." She smiled at him. All of her edginess and downtown cool had vanished. Rabbi had that effect on women. Gulliver might as well have not been there. When she became aware that she was staring, she spoke. "Now, if you'll excuse me, gentlemen..."

She retreated. Rabbi watched her go. Gulliver watched Rabbi watching her. His friend wasn't very choosy when it came to women. They all loved him, and he loved them all back. It was easy to figure out which one he was going to love tonight.

After she was gone, Rabbi said, "You know, Gullie, I was thinking about your parents today."

"Really? I thought you were thinking about boning the hostess. My guess is her favorite color is leather."

"Don't be an idiot, Gullie. Like I was saying, I was thinking about your parents today."

"My parents meant well. But meaning well wasn't enough. It all went wrong," Gulliver said. "Their beliefs were a mash-up of old folk songs and public-service announcements. They were going to change the world by being nice people. By adopting the runts of the litter that not even their own mothers could love."

"I loved your parents. They were the kindest people I ever met. It wasn't their fault that they were already old when they adopted you and Keisha."

"I know. I loved them too. But all their kindness earned them was an early grave."

Rabbi raised his glass. "To your folks."

"To my folks."

They clinked glasses and drank. Gulliver asked when they were going to get down to business. Rabbi said he wasn't sure.

"I never met the person hiring you. She is a friend of one of my biggest clients. All I was told was that she owns this place. That's all I know." Rabbi shrugged. "I'll call you tomorrow to see how it went. Take care of yourself."

As Rabbi left, Gulliver took a closer look around the Club Room. He stared at the coats of arms and the foxhunting scenes. A year from now no one would even remember that Black and Blue had been here, Gulliver thought. Some yahoo in a salvage yard in Pissville would be selling the Club Room panels. The coats of arms would end up in flea markets in Indiana. The foxhunting scenes would find new homes in interstate motel rooms.

In Manhattan everything was about what was hot. Tomorrow didn't matter. You could never be sure of tomorrow.

Then someone standing behind Gulliver's chair spoke. The world stopped turning. "Hello, Gullie."

The woman's voice cut a hole through Gulliver's chest and into his heart. He froze with panic. It couldn't be Nina. Not Nina, not after all this time. Nina, who seventeen years ago had given him love and hope for two months. It was the only love, the only hope, he had ever known. Then she had robbed him of both things as quickly as she had given them.

He could not bring himself to turn around. Because it might be her, or because it might not be? Not even he knew the answer. He had to look. He gathered up every ounce of strength he had and turned his head.

CHAPTER THREE

Nina Morton was even more beautiful now than she was as a teenager. She stood only two feet away from him. But it felt like seventeen years away. He was time traveling. It was again graduation day at Sachem North High School on Long Island. That was the last time he had seen her. All the anger and bitterness of that day welled up in him again. The tears too. He pushed them down. He would not let her see him cry. Not again.

He willed his hands not to shake. Nina had tried to speak to him on graduation day, after she had broken up with him. He would not listen then. He did not want to listen now. It was hard to listen with a broken heart. Seventeen years ago he had hobbled away from her as fast as he could. He had tripped over the hem of his graduation gown and fallen into a puddle. The other kids laughed at the mud on his face. One said, "Hey, Gulliver, now you look just like Keisha."

The cruel things the kids said that day didn't matter. He was bulletproof. No one could hurt him more than Nina had. Gulliver remembered something else about that day. It was Nina's old boyfriend Eddie who had helped him out of the mud. He remembered the sad look in Eddie's eyes. They had looked almost as sad as Gulliver felt.

"Leave him alone, Nina," Eddie had said, stepping between her and Gulliver. "You've already done enough damage."

His last memory of Nina was of her black graduation gown disappearing in the crowd.

He wanted to tell her how stupid in love with her he had been. Instead, he said, "You look vaguely familiar. So who are you again?"

"Nice try, Gullie. You still can't lie to me."

"You lost the right to call me Gullie seventeen years ago."

"Sorry, Gulliver. May I sit down?"

"Sit. What do I care? You own the place, right?"

"I do, yeah," she said.

Gulliver held down his anger. He watched Nina as she took Rabbi's seat. Much about her had changed. She was just a girl when he'd known her. She had remained unaged and unchanged in his heart. Now she was thirty-five. Womanhood agreed with her. Her bobbed black hair, coppery eyes, perfect nose and full lips still tugged at him. Her lush curves had deepened. Gulliver had run his hands over those curves thousands of times in his painful daydreams. The outlines of her legs had been further defined and sculpted by time. Nina knew how to make up. She knew how to dress. She wore a simple gray cocktail dress that fit her body the way white fits rice. Her light black stockings had a sexy seam that ran down the back of her legs and into killer black heels. Yet there was a sadness in her smile that he didn't recognize.

They sat silently across from one another. Each one was studying the other. Then she said, "I was very, very sorry to hear about Keisha."

"I guess your sympathy card got lost in the mail. Damned post office."

She bowed her head. "I didn't think you would want to hear from me."

"I didn't...I still don't," he lied.

Nina ignored that. "Besides, when did you ever want anybody's sympathy?"

She had a point. Like Rabbi, Nina had been able to look directly into Gulliver's teenage heart. He could hide nothing from her back then. And he guessed he wasn't doing it very well now. But Nina's gift was different than Rabbi's. Rabbi was kind of blind to Gulliver's looks. Nina wasn't blind to Gulliver at all. She had seen Gulliver for what he was. And for two months, seventeen years ago, Nina Morton had ignored his height and deformities. She ignored the whispers from her friends. She ignored the taunting of her rivals. She had walked the halls of Sachem North High School holding Gulliver Dowd's hand.

"Well, I was sorry to hear about Keisha. Whether you believe me or not. I liked her. You must have been very proud of her when she joined the police force."

Gulliver was being torn in half. He was twisted inside out. He wanted both to beg her for another chance and to spit in her face. He wanted to hold her. He wanted to run his hands over her curves. He wanted to gimp away and never look back. But he couldn't stand the pain of her bringing his dead sister into it.

"What's this about, Nina? You didn't arrange this meeting just to tell me you were sorry about Keisha. After all this time, what could you want from me? Did you want to kick me around a little more to feel important?"

"I need your help," she said. A lone tear slid down her left cheek.

Gulliver hissed, "Fuck you!"

"I guess I deserved that."

"You deserve a lot more than that. Did Rabbi have anything to do with this setup?"

"No. I worked through one of his clients. He's a man I..." She cleared her throat. "Let's just say I know him very well."

"What is that supposed to mean?" he asked.

She ignored him. "I need your help."

"Why, are you starting a freak show to compete with the one in Coney Island?"

"My daughter is missing."

"I don't do runaways," he lied again. Runaways were a big part of his business. Parents of missing children didn't care about his looks. Parents of missing children only cared about one thing—finding their children. "Just call the cops."

"I can't."

"Then find somebody else," he said.

"Her name's Anka."

Gulliver wouldn't budge. "Beautiful name. So what?"

"It's Polish for Hannah, your mother's name."

28

"My mother thanks you. If you want, I can recommend some—"

"She's sixteen, Gulliver." Nina's voice was sharp, brittle. "Do the math, you idiot. She's yours."

After a moment someone said, "Is she… normal?" It was Gulliver.

Nina handed him a photo. "She's perfect."

CHAPTER FOUR

The Wilton Academy was perched on a bluff above the Hudson River. It was about fifty miles north of New York City. The trees in the city were still lush and green. But the trees near Wilton had begun to change into their fall wardrobe. The view from the car window was a leafy rainbow. Bright yellows, deep reds, pale browns and a hundred shades of green. The blue skies with pillowy white clouds could make you believe that all was right with the world. But you would be wrong.

Gulliver's van was fitted with special equipment, so he was able to drive. But his head was still spinning from the news that he had a daughter. A beautiful, five-foot-seven-inch, blond-haired, blue-eyed daughter. One named after his own mother. His head was spinning because that new and perfect daughter was gone.

So instead of driving himself to the school that Anka attended, Gulliver went to Wilton with Ahmed Foster. Ahmed was the ex-Navy Seal who had taught him knife-fighting skills. He and Gulliver weren't friends, exactly. But they had known each other since high school. Ahmed had even dated Keisha for a time back then. Gulliver and Ahmed had met again at Keisha's funeral and formed a kind of team. Whenever Gulliver needed someone to help on a case, he hired Ahmed. He was built like a linebacker. He had a face that was as rough as the side of a cliff.

He also had a cold stare that scared the hell out of folks. With Ahmed around, people paid less attention to Gulliver than usual.

The Wilton Academy did not accept everyone. Not even if their families were rich and powerful. So Gulliver's newfound daughter was not only even prettier than her mother, she was also really smart. She was a very gifted artist too. After Nina had told him about Anka the night before, she'd taken Gulliver to her office. She'd shown him all of their daughter's report cards. She'd shown him photo albums. All the pictures were of Anka. The first ones were of Anka as a baby. The newest ones were taken at her last birthday party. The walls of Nina's office were decorated with Anka's artwork. There were paintings, photographs and figure drawings.

"These are incredible," Gulliver had said, staring at his daughter's artwork. "Amazing!"

But not everything had gone so smoothly.

"Why didn't you tell me the truth until now?" Gulliver had asked, his voice full of anger.

"I didn't tell anyone the truth. After a while I began to believe the lies myself. I wanted the baby, Gulliver. But if my parents had known you were the father..."

Nina didn't need to say another word. Gulliver understood. Her parents would not have let her have a child that could turn out looking like a garden gnome. It hurt to think that. But it was the truth. And he never turned away from the truth.

Nina went on, "It was hard enough to convince them to let me keep the baby. No matter who the father was."

"Funny you should mention that. Who did you tell them the father was? Eddie?"

Nina looked sick. "No. I had broken up with Eddie by then. You knew that.

They knew that. I told them I'd faked my way into a bar in Smithtown. I said I got really drunk and slept with some guy I met there. I said I didn't know his name. That he was visiting from out of state. They believed it because they wanted to believe it."

"You mean, as long as it wasn't me," Gulliver said.

She couldn't look him in the eye. "Yes... as long as it wasn't you."

"But after you moved out of the house and had the baby...why didn't you tell me then?"

"Because she was mine, Gulliver. I raised her. I managed to get through college and everything. Just Anka and me, with a little help from my aunt in Boulder. I went to school out there. No one else was a part of our lives. And like I said, I began to believe my own lies. It was easier to pretend her father was some nameless guy I screwed in a bar parking lot. It was less painful that way. Sure, I thought of telling you over the years. But I thought you hated me for breaking up with you on graduation day."

"You were right. I did hate you. I do."

"I had to do it. To hide the pregnancy from you. After that the timing never seemed right. There isn't a right time to tell someone that kind of secret."

"But you're telling me now," he said.

"Only because I have to. I'm scared. I will do anything, Gulliver...anything to get her back."

He shook his head. "Anything but go to the police."

"I can't," Nina said. "I own this steakhouse. But I borrowed the money for it. And not from a bank."

"You idiot," Gulliver screamed at her. "You borrowed it from loan sharks!"

"Not exactly. I borrowed it directly from Joey Vespucci."

"Joey 'Dollar Menu' Vespucci! The guy who runs what's left of the mob in New York?" Vespucci was nicknamed Dollar Menu because he loved fast food.

"I've known Joey for many years," she said. "We did other business together. He loaned me the money at very low interest. I just had to front some other businesses of his."

"What other businesses?"

Nina turned away. "Clubs."

"Clubs?"

"Do I have to spell it out for you, Gulliver?"

"Gentlemen's clubs, sex clubs," he said. "But what does any of this have to do with Anka going missing?"

"This place is doing great. And I got a legitimate loan to pay off the note and to pay Joey back all the money he loaned me."

"Let me guess, Nina. When you paid him back, you asked if he would let you get off the paperwork from the other places. That you didn't want to front for him anymore. He told you to take a hike. You acted all tough. You told him you would go to the cops if you had to. Then he threatened you. He probably had a file with Anka's picture in it. He knew where she went to school and everything. Am I close?"

"It was exactly like that," she said. "It's like you were there. Do you see why I can't go to the cops? If Joey's got her, he'll kill her."

"How could you let yourself get into business with a wiseguy? Once they have you, they never let you go."

"I knew him from before. I trusted him. I couldn't let the opportunity to buy this place get away. It would mean I could finally get out from under. I could send Anka to school anywhere she wanted. She could live a life that I never could. She could be free in a way I never was."

Gulliver sneered. "Yeah, look where that kind of freedom's gotten her."

"Find her," Nina said. Her voice was soft.

Then she unzipped her gray dress. She dropped it to reveal a silken black bra, a matching thong and garter belt. She undid her bra. It fell at her feet. Her breasts were fuller than he remembered. Her nipples, dark and erect. She moved close to Gulliver. She reached for his jacket.

"Find her, Gullie. Like I said, I'll do anything. Let me show you."

He stepped back, slapping her hands away.

"For almost twenty years, Nina, I've dreamed of us being together again. In spite of how you broke my heart. I imagined a million scenes of us in bed together. Sometimes, after Keisha died, the only thing that made life worth living was thinking about us back together. Now you just make me sick."

He grabbed a small leather case from his jacket pocket. He took out a business card and put it on her desk.

"Email or fax me about her school and who I should talk to. I will deal with Joey Dollar Menu at the proper time. But first get me that stuff."

As he walked past her, Nina said, "I'm sorry, Gullie. I'm desperate. I just don't know what else to do."

He said nothing, just kept walking to the door.

"Where are you going?" Nina called after him.

"To forget my past and think about my future," Gulliver said. He'd slammed the office door shut behind him.

Now Gulliver could not get the image of Nina's half-naked body out of his head. No matter how furious he was with her, he was still in love with her. It hadn't been easy to turn his back on what she had offered. Maybe when he found his daughter, he would see if they could try again. Maybe then Gulliver would see if there was anything left between Nina and him. Maybe then he would let Nina show her gratitude.

Ahmed turned off the country lane. Gulliver knew he had to stop daydreaming about Nina. Only one thing mattered now. Anka. Ahmed drove through the gated archway. He drove past the tall stone walls that surrounded the campus of the Wilton Academy. He came to a stop on the gravel driveway in front of the main building. It was a massive red-brick manor house that had been turned into a school building. Tall columns supported an arch of concrete and stone. Ivy crawled over the walls. It was hard to see the red brick beneath.

Before they had even gotten out of Ahmed's pearly-white Escalade, a frumpy elderly woman was heading down the steps toward them.

"That's one unhappy-lookin' lady," Ahmed said.

"Missing girls are bad for business. Come on, let's go see what there is to see. When I'm inside with Miss Sunshine, you go have a chat with security."

"I know the drill, little man. You do your thing. I'll do mine. The brothers'll talk to me."

CHAPTER FIVE

Gulliver had never believed people really had names like Muffy and Jocasta. But he would have to change his mind about that now.

Miss Sunshine held her hand out and down to Gulliver. She said, "A pleasure, Mr. Dowd. I am Dr. Cissy Fenn Chatsworth, headmistress of the Wilton Academy."

"A pleasure," he repeated. He gave her papery hand a soft shake.

She looked as if she wanted to wash her hand after Gulliver had shaken it. Gulliver noticed. He had the urge to tell her not to worry. That what he had wasn't catching. He kept his mouth shut because he needed this woman's help. He couldn't risk angering her. Not yet.

Dr. Chatsworth showed him into her office. She forced him to have some tea with her. Then she gave him Anka's file. "She was a wonderful student, a true star of her class."

She went on about how bright Anka was. What a talented artist she was. She showed him Anka's test results from the previous year. She gave him all of the instructors' glowing student evaluations. But there was a strange tone in her voice. It sounded a lot like pity. He knew the sound of pity better than any man alive. There was something else that didn't escape Gulliver's notice.

"Dr. Chatsworth. I notice you keep referring to Anka in the past tense. You are perfectly happy to discuss last year. But you haven't said a word about what's been going on this year."

"I'm afraid it is a very old story, Mr. Dowd," Dr. Chatsworth sighed. "Girls come to us bright and full of promise. Then they make the wrong sorts of friends or discover boys and...This year Anka returned from her summer vacation a different girl. She was angry and uncooperative. She did only C work. She didn't seem at all interested in any of her clubs. Yes, as I say, a very old story. You are not the first person to come here looking for a missing girl, Mr. Dowd. Nor will you be the last."

"I'm not worried about them right now. I'm worried about Anka."

"I understand."

"Did Anka have the *wrong* sorts of friends? Had she discovered boys?" he asked.

"I could not say. She refused to discuss her problems with us. A pity, too. Had she continued her behavior, we would have had to dismiss her. In any case, with all the social media and networking...it's quite impossible for us to keep track of what our girls get into."

There wasn't anything left for Dr. Chatsworth to say. She showed him Anka's room. It had posters of rock and movie stars. A jewelry box. A dresser, a half-empty closet. Some of her photos and paintings on the walls. Gulliver could feel her presence. The headmistress introduced Gulliver to Anka's suitemates, some friends. Her teachers, the school psychologist. All told a similar story. That something must have happened to Anka over the summer. That she came back to school a very different girl than the one who had left in June.

"She was pissed about something," one suitemate said.

"And hurt bad," said another.

The school shrink agreed. "Angry, yes, but I think more wounded than angry."

Gulliver got pretty much the same story from everyone. Anka had gone to all of her classes on Thursday. She had skipped dinner and gone to bed around eleven. She didn't attend her first two classes the next day. So the school had sent someone to check on her. By then she was gone. No note. But no sign of a struggle either. She had apparently just left at some point during the night. They had contacted Nina immediately. She had told them not to call the police. That it was a family matter and that she would see to it.

Gulliver had done this many times before. He knew that everyone lies a little bit. He knew Anka's friends had more to say. They just hadn't wanted to say it in front of Dr. Chatsworth. Teenagers liked to talk to Gulliver. They felt on the inside the way he looked on the outside. He thought that maybe even the school shrink had wanted to say more than she dared to in front of her boss. He knew how to handle that too. He had his ways. He'd be back if he needed to. Before leaving, he asked Dr. Chatsworth to let him see Anka's room one last time. The headmistress didn't see the point, but Gulliver didn't care.

He stood at the center of his daughter's room. He took slow, deep breaths, trying to see things that hadn't been obvious to him earlier. This was a trick his karate teacher had shown him. It was like going into a trance that let him focus his attention. He moved his gaze from one part of the room to another. His eyes kept returning to Anka's closet and the jewelry box on her dresser. He knew that what kids left behind could be as important as what they took. If he had had the time, Gulliver would have listed each item in the closet and the jewelry box. Instead, he took a photo of the things hanging in Anka's closet. He dumped the contents of the jewelry box in his jacket pockets. Was this strictly legal? No, but this was his daughter who was missing. And he meant to find her no matter what.

"Will you be returning to the campus, Mr. Dowd?" Dr. Chatsworth asked. "Having someone like you about is very upsetting to the girls."

"Someone like me?"

"An investigator," she said. But Gulliver knew that was only half true.

He smiled and answered. Also with a half-truth. "No, I don't think I'll be back."

Gulliver was right. Everyone lies a little bit. Him too.

"Mr. Dowd, please tell Anka's mother not to worry. Her daughter's not the first girl to try to run away from her problems. Sadly, the problems stay with them. When Anka realizes this, she'll turn up. They always do."

Gulliver didn't like this woman's smugness. He never liked people who thought they had all the answers. "What makes you certain Anka ran away?"

Dr. Chatsworth looked at Gulliver as if he was a fool. "What else could it be?"

"I don't know," he said. "That's why I'm here. To find out."

"I hope you are not implying that we are the cause for what has taken place."

"Aren't you?" He kept at her. "Anka was under your care, in your school."

Now Dr. Cissy Fenn Chatsworth's papery skin turned bright red. Her mouth moved, but no words came out.

Gulliver enjoyed watching the old biddy. But he had to get going. "Good day, Dr. Chatsworth. A pleasure."

With that, he turned on his heel and headed back to the Escalade.

CHAPTER SIX

Questions swirled in Gulliver's head as Ahmed drove back to the city. *Did Anka just pick up and go?* He didn't want to admit it. But it did look like Anka had run away. The question was, why? Was it because of something that had happened over the summer break? If so, what?

Gulliver laughed to himself. He'd been a father for less than twenty-four hours. And he was already confused and angry. He guessed that made him like most fathers of teenage girls. He could picture himself asking Anka's prom date into his office.

Cleaning his gun in front of the kid. *Be nice to my little girl or else.* He laughed again. Gulliver had always heard that parenthood changes you. Now he knew it was true.

"What's so funny, little man?" Ahmed asked. Gulliver didn't mind Ahmed calling him that as long as it wasn't in front of other people.

"Nothing. Just thinking." Gulliver hadn't told Ahmed that he was Anka's father. He wasn't going to tell anyone. Not yet. Things were already complicated enough. When he found Anka, he would shout his pride to the world. But that was for later. He asked Ahmed, "What did security tell you?"

"Most of them told me nothing. But there's always an unhappy one in the bunch."

"And you found him?"

Ahmed nodded. "I always do."

"So far you're batting a thousand. Tell me."

"Skinny white boy named Henry. Washed out of some punkass Putnam

51

County police department. He beat a guy up at a traffic stop. Henry's got a chip on his shoulder bigger than his shoulder. Don't like taking orders from people."

Gulliver was curious. "What did he say?"

"Said this Anka girl caught everybody's eye. If you know what I'm sayin'. Hot, but a good girl. No trouble. Henry said he thought she had a boyfriend at Bloomfield Prep. A mile or two away from Wilton."

Gulliver said, "I figured she must've had a boyfriend. So there's nothing there."

"I didn't say that. Did I say that? Seems a few of the girls reported seeing an older man hangin' around just outside the campus. He had cameras and such. Henry saw the man. Tried to chase him off. The older man wouldn't go. He said he was on public land. Said he was bird-watchin'. Henry thinks he was bird-watchin', all right. That bird was named Anka Morton. Guy had a camera on a tripod. Henry looked through it. It was aimed at Anka's dorm-room window."

"Was it reported to the local cops?" Gulliver asked.

"It was. But like the guy said, he was on public land."

"Did Henry get the man's name?"

"Nah. Guy refused to give it. There wasn't nothin' Henry could do about that."

"Maybe it was nothing." Gulliver didn't really believe what he had just said.

Ahmed shook his head. "That's what Henry thought too. Then he was in town one day when he was off duty. He saw that guy comin' out of the local coffee shop. When Henry went inside, Anka was sittin' at a table for two. There was a wrapped-up gift box in a shopping bag next to the table. The girl was, like, all smiley and shit."

"Maybe Henry was reading too much into it, Ahmed. Maybe they both just happened to be there at the same time."

"Sorry, little man, but no. Coffee shop was empty 'cept for Anka. The only table in use was that two-top. He had definitely been at that table with her. I'm thinkin' he's a predator. You know. Chats her up online and then starts bringin' her gifts and all. Next time maybe they ain't meetin' at no coffee shop, but at the local no-tell motel."

"Could be. Or maybe he was setting her up for something else."

Ahmed didn't get it. "Somethin' else. Like what?"

"Never mind that. Did Henry tell you what the guy looked like?"

"White, thirty-five or forty. About six foot tall, two hundred pounds. Light brown hair. Blue eyes."

"Okay," Gulliver said. "Head to Staten Island."

"Staten Island! What's in Staten Island besides that big closed-down garbage dump?"

"Joey Vespucci."

"You crazy, Gulliver? That man ain't gonna talk to you."

"How much money did it take to get Henry to talk to you?"

"A hundred bucks," Ahmed said. "Why?"

"Double or nothing. If Joey Dollar Menu will see me, you lose the hundred. If the man refuses, you get the hundred back plus another hundred on top."

Ahmed removed his right hand from the steering wheel. He offered it to Gulliver. "It's a bet."

Gulliver shook it. "Staten Island, here we come."

CHAPTER SEVEN

For years the Todt Hill area of Staten Island had been a favorite of the mob. Gulliver wondered if the mob boys knew that *todt* meant dead in Dutch. He doubted it. The wiseguys Gulliver knew weren't keen on learning Dutch. Or the deeper meanings of things. The Mafia types he met were focused on three things. Making money. Staying out of prison. And staying alive. Since the mid-1980s, all of those things were harder to do. The Mafia was still alive and kicking. Just not as alive or as kicking as it once had been. The code of silence that had kept the big bosses out of the law's reach was a thing of the past.

The only big boss left with a high profile was Joey Vespucci. The other bosses were like ghosts. You didn't see their names in the papers. You didn't see them on TV. They lived quietly, in tasteful houses far away from the old neighborhoods.

That wasn't Joey Vespucci's way. He made sure the world knew who he was. He lived in a huge house. It was much bigger than the rest of the houses on his street. Not only was his home too large, it was ugly. It looked like a mix between a stucco castle, a fast-food restaurant and a strip club. The lawn was dotted with concrete statues of busty nude women, forest creatures and religious icons. Gulliver doubted Vespucci could be any more tasteless if he tried.

Ahmed parked around the corner. They didn't want to draw attention to themselves. But good luck with that. A well-muscled black man and a white dwarf rolling up to a front gate in a Cadillac Escalade get noticed. Gulliver walked around the corner. He walked right up to Joey's wrought-iron gate and pressed the buzzer on the intercom. He waved at the camera perched on one of the stone gateposts.

"Go away, kid. We ain't buying no candy for your team," a gravelly voice ordered.

"Listen, asshole, I'm not a kid. The name's Dowd, and I'm here to see Mr. Vespucci."

There was a burst of laughter. Then, "Mr. Vespucci don't wanna see you. He don't like circus freaks. They make him all hinky. Now get the fuck outta here before I come out there and squish ya."

"Tell Mr. Vespucci I'm here about Nina Morton. He can call her to check. I'll wait."

But he didn't have to wait. There was a buzz. The gate clicked open. It swung back. Gulliver stepped through. The gate snapped shut behind him. He waddled up the long walkway to the house. A barrel-chested man with no neck and a round face stepped out onto the porch. Gulliver could see the holster bulge in the guy's ill-fitting but expensive suit jacket. Wearing a gun doesn't make a guy tough. The bulge just made it easier to take his weapon away from him. Gulliver was carrying a 9mm SIG Sauer, but no one would know it to look at him. He expected to get patted down. It didn't happen. Mr. No Neck just let him walk by.

"Walk straight ahead into the study," No Neck ordered.

Gulliver couldn't resist asking, "What's Mr. Vespucci studying in there?"

"Shut up, bug, and walk."

Sitting behind a large, fancy desk was Joey Vespucci. Gulliver knew he would have to gain Joey's respect to get his attention. That wasn't always easy to do. Some people were hard to convince. With them, it could take a few meetings. Gulliver didn't have the luxury of time. Good thing Mr. No Neck was about to let Gulliver prove himself.

"You should be more careful about who you let guard your life," Gulliver said to Joey before the mob boss could speak. "This clown here will get you killed someday."

No Neck laughed. "Look who's calling who a clown."

That was Gulliver's cue. He dropped to his knee. He reached under his jacket and spun. Before either Vespucci or his goon could react, Gulliver was pointing his 9mm at Joey's head.

"What the fuck!" Mr. No Neck shouted, loudly enough to draw attention.

They heard pounding footsteps down the hallway. Gulliver could have blown Joey's head off and shot No Neck in the liver. He could have been ready to wipe out anyone coming through the study door. Instead, Gulliver dropped the clip out of the gun's handle. He ejected the bullet in the chamber and set the 9mm on Joey's desk. He held his hands over his head. But he knew this wasn't over. These weren't the type of men to laugh off this kind of thing.

No Neck charged. Gulliver waited until the big man was almost on him. Then he stepped to his left and raised his right leg. He threw a chopping kick at the goon's right knee. No Neck crumpled to the carpeting. He howled in pain. Gulliver clamped his hand around the goon's right thumb and locked it. He had been amazed at this when he learned the technique. *Control your enemy's thumb and you control your enemy*, his karate teacher had said. For now Gulliver only wanted to impress his enemy's boss. He twisted No Neck's arm behind him. He took No Neck's gun and held his knife to his throat.

Gulliver had proved his point. He dropped the knife, let go of the goon and again raised his arms.

Vespucci watched it all with a semi-amused scowl on his face.

"Like I said, Mr. Vespucci, you ought to be more careful."

"Get outta here, you moron," Vespucci shouted at Mr. No Neck. "Take the little man's weapons and give 'em back when he leaves."

No Neck wasn't pleased. But he followed his master's orders like a good dog.

"Okay, little man, you got my attention," Vespucci said. "What do you want with it?"

"First thing I want is for you to not call me little man."

Vespucci's lip started to curl in an angry sneer. He wasn't used to people correcting him. He wasn't used to someone like Gulliver doing anything but kissing his ass. But then the sneer vanished. Vespucci said, "You got some balls on you, little— sorry. You got some balls on you, Dowd. I respect that."

Gulliver bowed his head slightly. "Thank you, Mr. Vespucci."

"So, you know Nina, huh?"

Gulliver smiled. "Since we were kids in Lake Ronkonkoma on Long Island, yeah."

"Then maybe you can talk some sense into her, Dowd. She's taking some chances she shouldn't be taking."

"Funny thing. I think she hoped I could talk some sense into you."

Vespucci was a slender, handsome man in his early sixties, with a sharp jawline and graying hair. He shook his head in disbelief. His brown eyes were on fire. It was one thing for this dwarf to have balls. It was something else for him to give Vespucci trouble. He stood up and came around the big desk.

"What sort of sense does Nina want you to talk into me?" he asked in a threatening voice.

"Her sixteen-year-old daughter's missing. Nina thinks you might have her."

"Why's she think that?"

Gulliver said, "Because you threatened her when she told you she didn't want to front for you anymore."

Vespucci's body stiffened. As smoothly as a cat, he grabbed some framed photos from the fireplace mantel. "See these here?" he barked, shoving the frames at Gulliver. "These are my daughters and my grand-kids. You think I would take Nina's kid just because she's pissing me off?"

"I know only what I read in the papers, Mr. Vespucci. I know you've had people killed. And to get to where you are, I know you've killed people yourself."

"You take some chances, Dowd. Some big chances. Talking to me like that in my house."

"Maybe, Mr. Vespucci. I didn't survive this long by being afraid. I'm here because Nina's daughter is my daughter too. So I'll risk whatever I have to find her. I didn't find out she was my kid until last night. I want to know her more than I have ever wanted anything. For me, that's saying a lot. I think maybe you can understand." Gulliver held Vespucci's photos out to him. "If your girls were in danger, wouldn't you take risks?"

"Okay, I understand now." Vespucci replaced the pictures on the mantel. "But I ain't got the kid. I swear on the life of my own girls and grandkids. You gotta believe I wouldn't do that."

"But you threatened Nina that you would, Mr. Vespucci."

"I did, but that's all it was. Nina's been around long enough to know how this stuff works. You don't pull out on me when it suits you. She knew that going in. Still, I wouldn't hurt her kid. I wouldn't hurt nobody's kid. She knows that. I'm surprised she sent you here. I'm surprised by a lot of things."

Gulliver understood. "Nina and I dated for around two months when we were seniors in high school. Then she broke up with me on graduation day. She left for the University of Colorado. I didn't see her again until last night."

"That's when she told you about the girl," Joey said.

"Yeah. I'm a licensed PI. I do a lot of missing-kids work."

"You sure as shit can handle yourself. I'll give you that, Dowd. I've seen Tony beat the crap out of guys a foot taller than him. You made him look silly. But I don't have the girl." Vespucci crossed his heart. "If you need some info you can't get elsewhere, just let me know. I'll get it for you. We understand each other?" Vespucci said. He put out his right hand.

Gulliver shook it. "I understand. I may take you up on it."

"Look, Dowd, I got a heart. I just can't afford to let anyone know it. I'm going to do something now that I'm probably going to regret. But hey, sometimes a little compassion is a good thing. Right?"

"I guess that's why my parents adopted me. So what are you going to regret, Mr. Vespucci?"

"You tell Nina she's out of it. She can have what she wants. I'll have my lawyer draw up the papers. Tell her I hope she gets the kid back. You too, Dowd. I hope you find your kid. I have boys too, but a daughter is special." He was staring at the photos on the mantel. "They are really special."

"Thanks, Mr. Vespucci. You're right. I don't know her, but I know she's special."

"Do me a favor, Dowd. Call me Joey. Not many people call me that. I kinda miss hearing it."

"It's a deal, Joey," Gulliver said.

Vespucci was still staring at the mantel. "I'll tell Tony not to bust your balls on the way out."

As Gulliver turned to go, Vespucci called after him. "Just one last thing. Watch your back with Nina. I've known her for going on fourteen years. She isn't always what she seems."

"How's that?"

"Ask Nina how I know her. Then you'll understand. Take care, little man." He winked when he said it. Gulliver smiled.

Gulliver liked Joey Vespucci. He knew he shouldn't, because Joey was a killer. But life was crazy that way. Gulliver hated some people he knew he should like. He liked some people he knew he should hate.

In the hallway outside the study, Mr. No Neck waited for Gulliver. He gave him back his SIG and knife. Mr. No Neck wasn't confused about his feelings. He hated Gulliver. That wasn't going to change.

CHAPTER EIGHT

Ahmed drove away from Todt Hill and headed back to Brooklyn. After Keisha's murder, Gulliver had left Long Island. He'd moved into the loft space his little sister had bought in Red Hook. Red Hook had once been the toughest neighborhood in New York City. Now it was kind of hip. But it wasn't quite tamed. First Keisha and now Gulliver liked it that way. Red Hook reflected their lives—orphaned, rough around the edges, but good at heart.

Ahmed told Gulliver he had done a little phone work. He had gotten the name of

Anka's boyfriend at Bloomfield Prep. From what Ahmed had heard, Dillon Kent was a good kid. A smart kid.

"That all you got?" Gulliver asked.

Ahmed grinned. "So far…except maybe his cell-phone number."

"And how'd you manage that?"

"Hey, little man, you've got your ways, I've got mine."

Gulliver agreed. "Fair enough. What's the number?"

Ahmed remained silent. Gulliver repeated the question several times. Then it hit him. "Oh, the bet about Vespucci not seeing me. You owe me how much? A hundred on top of the hundred I don't have to give back to you? Okay. You give me Dillon Kent's cell number. I'll forget about the second hundred you owe me."

Ahmed pretended not to hear. "Did you say somethin', little man, or is there, like, a mosquito buzzin' in my ear?"

Gulliver gave up. He handed five twenty-dollar bills to Ahmed. "All right, we'll make it like the bet never existed."

Gulliver entered Dillon Kent's number into his cell phone. He didn't press the Call button. Gulliver had reached his limit for the day. And talking to high schoolers could be delicate. Their hormones and emotions ran high all the time. One false step, and you could lose them. One wrong question, and you might lose their goodwill. There were many reasons Gulliver would never ever want to go back to high school. Just recalling how intensely he had felt everything back then was enough to make him feel sick to his stomach.

Mostly what he'd felt in those days was shame and anger. The pain of his high-school years was never going to go away fully. It was etched into him. Working this case was bringing it all back to him. He was having a hard time controlling his feelings.

He was being pushed and pulled in all directions. He needed to go home to rest. To collect his thoughts before going back to see Nina.

"Drop me off at Visitation Place, Ahmed," Gulliver said. He looked out the window at the Statue of Liberty.

"Will you need me anymore today or tomorrow?"

"Not tonight. Maybe tomorrow. We'll talk in the morning."

Ahmed pulled the Escalade up in front of Gulliver's building. Gulliver hopped out without a word. He stood on the sidewalk in front of the old factory building. No wonder Keisha had picked this place. He stared up at the chipped brick. At the cracked door glass. At the worn steps. This place was like them. It was like Red Hook. Worn down. Beaten up. Not defeated.

CHAPTER NINE

Gulliver thought about going to talk with Nina at the restaurant again. He asked Rabbi to join him. His old friend turned him down. He said that he and the hostess hadn't really hit it off. The sex had been fine. Better than fine. There was just no spark between them.

He had heard Rabbi's tale of woe countless times before. It usually didn't faze him. Gulliver had been without love for so long, he'd grown almost numb. But seeing Nina again had changed all that. The image of Nina nude before him brought alive feelings that had lain sleeping in his heart for many years.

He now remembered the drunken power of love. The simple joy in the touch and scent of a woman. He remembered how for two brief months he had been able to shut out the pain. How it had seemed there wasn't anything he couldn't do. That as long as he had Nina's love, there was no challenge he couldn't face.

Now Gulliver lost patience with his old friend. Women threw themselves at Rabbi and he threw them back. How Gulliver ached sometimes to be so lucky.

He decided to call Nina instead of going to the restaurant. He had his reasons. For one, he didn't want to deal with the hostess again. She hadn't exactly been warm to him. And that was before Rabbi had slept with her. But even Gulliver knew that wasn't the main reason.

The truth was, he didn't think he could turn Nina down a second time. If she offered herself again, he would say yes. He had struggled all day with his decision to walk away from her after all his years of longing. The picture of her in his mind had haunted him as he toured the Wilton Academy. It had haunted him in Joey Vespucci's study and on the ride back to Red Hook. It haunted him now as he held the phone in his hand.

Nina's voice was all business. "Did you find her?"

"No, but I made some progress. Did you know she has a boyfriend?"

"Dillon Kent," she said. "He comes from a very good family."

"So what does that mean? Good family means rich family. Some of the most fucked-up people I've ever met are from *good* families. Why didn't you tell me about him?"

"Relax, Gullie, he's a good kid. I already spoke to him. He had nothing to do with Anka's disappearance."

Gulliver wasn't buying it. "How can you be sure?"

"Go see for yourself."

"I intend to. Tomorrow morning."

"I'll call ahead to the school," Nina offered. "I still don't think you'll—"

"Look, Nina, let me do my job. Even if the kid is in the clear, he may know something you didn't know how to ask about."

"Like what?"

"Like the older man Anka was seeing," Gulliver said.

There were several seconds of silence on the other end of the phone. "What older man?"

"That's what I'm trying to find out. Security spotted an older man hanging around campus. Then a security guard ran into Anka and this guy at a local coffee shop."

She repeated her question. "What older man?"

"If I knew, Nina, I'd tell you. That's why I'm heading back up to the area around Wilton and Bloomfield Prep tomorrow. The people at Anka's school seem to think she ran away. Did you know. They think she got involved with something she couldn't handle. Started screwing up in school and split."

"But you don't think so?" Nina asked.

"I don't know enough yet to think anything. By the way, did something happen over the summer with Anka?"

"No!" Nina answered too loudly and too quickly. "Why?"

"Everyone at the school says she came back from summer vacation a different girl."

Nina changed the subject. "Did you check on Joey Vespucci?"

"Why are you so sure he has something to do with this, Nina?" Gulliver was curious.

"He threatened me. He threatened Anka."

"He doesn't have her," Gulliver said.

"How can you know that?"

"I had a long talk with him at his house today. Let's just say I believe him when he says he doesn't have her. You either have to trust me on that or hire someone else." Gulliver's threat was an empty threat. There was no way he was going to abandon a search for his daughter. Still, Nina backed down.

"Okay," she said. "Okay."

Gulliver opened his mouth to tell Nina the good news. That Joey Vespucci was going to let her off the hook. That she could go about running her restaurant in peace. But he didn't say a word. There was something in Nina's tone that Gulliver didn't like. He already didn't like that Nina hadn't gone to the cops. There were things she wasn't telling him. He seemed to be the only one who wasn't holding anything back. And that left him in a weaker place.

Well, that was going to change. In spite of his anger and hurt. In spite of all his pain and resentment, Gulliver Dowd always played it straight with people. His body might be twisted up, but he spoke the truth. He hoped other people would play it the same way. But when they played dirty, Gulliver could play that way too. He was low to the ground and more used to the dirt than the people who tried to play him for a fool.

CHAPTER TEN

They met off campus at the coffee shop in town. The minute Gulliver saw Dillon Kent, he understood that Nina was right about him. Dillon was a tall kid with an athletic build. He had unruly brown hair and an attractive face. He was wearing his school's uniform. Maroon blazer with gold trim, a fancy crest on the pocket. Beige slacks. White shirt. Gold-and-maroon-striped tie. The thing was, Dillon Kent was blind. The chocolate Labrador at his side was like the boy's fifth limb.

Gulliver called out, "Over here, Dillon!"

The kid turned his head to Gulliver. He navigated his way to the little booth in back with no trouble at all. When he arrived, he held his hand out. The hand was a little too high.

"Mr. Dowd?"

Gulliver pulled it down to his level and gave Dillon's hand a firm shake.

"I'm quite a bit shorter than you might have thought," Gulliver said.

The kid smirked and slid into the booth. "And I'm probably a bit blinder than you expected."

"Just a bit," Gulliver said. They both laughed. "Should we get your dog some water or something?"

"Her name's Cocoa. She prefers decaf coffee, orange juice, and eggs over easy with hot sauce."

"A comedian, huh?" Gulliver said. "Does Anka like that about you?"

Dillon winced at the mention of Anka. "I think she just liked Cocoa."

Gulliver backed off. They ordered breakfast. The two of them talked about everything but Anka. Were the Jets ever going to win another Super Bowl? Was the economy going to recover? Stuff like that. Then they talked about Dillon's blindness. He'd been that way since birth. There was nothing to be done about it.

"Money can protect you from everything except fate," he said. "I'm not bitter. This is the only life I know."

Gulliver liked that, even if he didn't feel the same way about things. He guessed he was plenty bitter for the both of them. They got back to talking about Anka. They both knew they would.

"Dillon, I hate asking you this. Was Anka—"

"Seeing someone else?" He finished Gulliver's question. He shifted in the booth enough that even Cocoa took notice. "You mean, was she cheating on me?"

"That's what I mean."

"This is going to sound foolish and maybe stupid, Mr. Dowd. But yes and no. I think there was somebody else. But I don't think she was cheating."

"I'm pretty smart, kid. Just not that smart. Do you mind explaining that one to me?"

Dillon repeated what everyone before him had said. That Anka had come back from summer vacation a changed person. He'd asked her about it, but she wouldn't discuss it. Whatever it was, it was big.

"When we were together..." Dillon said, blushing. "You know...together?"

"In bed." Gulliver gritted his teeth. The notion of teenagers fooling around didn't usually bother him. But Anka was his daughter.

"Yes, when we were in bed. I never felt like she wasn't there. We were good together.

And when we were alone like that, it was even better than before she left for the summer. But her head was somewhere else the rest of the time. Like there was something or someone on her mind. It was like she couldn't stop thinking about it. She wouldn't let me help her."

"Did she say anything at all, kid?"

"Only once, a few days before she split. She said she felt betrayed."

"Did she say by whom?"

"No."

"Did you tell Anka's mother about this?"

Dillon seemed surprised. "Of course. I want Anka back safely as much as anyone. More."

"I believe you, kid, I believe you. How did Anka's mother react when you told her about the betrayal?"

"I'm blind, Mr. Dowd."

"Good point, kid. How did her voice sound? What did she say?"

"She didn't really say much. I guess I could tell she didn't like hearing it."

That was pretty much where their conversation ended. Dillon offered to help Gulliver any way he could, even with money. "My family has more of it than they can spend. And believe me, they try. Let me help if you need money, Mr. Dowd."

Just as they were shaking hands goodbye, there was a tremendous explosion behind the coffee shop. The floor shook beneath their feet. Cocoa jumped up.

"Will you be all right, Dillon?" Gulliver asked. "Do you need me to help you outside?"

"I'm fine. Cocoa will get me out. And I have a driver waiting in front."

Gulliver didn't wait. He headed out of the coffee shop and around back as fast as he could move. It wasn't fast enough. Just as he had feared, his specially equipped van was engulfed in flames.

The stink of burning plastic and tires was overwhelming. The wind was blowing the black smoke directly into Gulliver's face. Through the smoke, he saw a man running in the opposite direction. Gulliver didn't think twice about following him. He took off after the running man.

It was at times like these that he hated himself most. There were things in his life he had overcome by the sheer force of will and guts. But there were some things, like stubby, uneven legs, that no amount of will and guts could change. No matter how hard he pushed, the gap between himself and the man ahead of him kept growing. At least it wasn't as large or increasing as fast as Gulliver had thought it might. In fact, this guy wasn't much faster than Gulliver. *He's not young*, Gulliver thought, *and probably not in great shape.*

Then the gap began to narrow. The running man was slowing down. Then he stopped. He was bent over. He was grabbing at his side. Gulliver knew that pain. He was feeling it himself. A stitch in his side that felt like someone was beating his ribs with a nine iron. When the man turned around and saw Gulliver gaining on him, he took off again. Gulliver got a blurry glimpse of him. The man's hair was light brown with wispy strands of gray. *Was this the man the security guard had seen on the grounds of the Wilton Academy? Was this the man who had been in the coffee shop with Anka?*

Now it was Gulliver's turn to stop to catch his breath. He was nauseous and more than a little dizzy. After a few seconds, he felt like he could breathe again. He wasn't dizzy anymore. When his stomach had settled down, Gulliver started after the man. He pushed himself to ignore the pain in his side.

There he is! The running man was walking now. He probably thought Gulliver had given up the chase. He was only three quarters of a block ahead and seemed to be in no hurry at all. Gulliver ducked into a doorway. He took in big gulps of air for a final sprint. The short time he spent there felt like forever.

Then Gulliver crossed the street, so the man wouldn't spot him as easily. He sped up enough to gain a little ground with every short stride. He thought there was something familiar about the guy. It was almost like he knew him. But he didn't. He couldn't. Still, he had a feeling he just could not shake. He would find out soon enough.

Now the man was less than a quarter of a block away. Gulliver decided to make his move. He checked to his left for oncoming traffic. None. His path was clear. But he hadn't checked for bicycles coming the wrong way down the street. *Bang!*

Gulliver went down in a heap. The bicycle's front wheel locked up. The Chinese-food delivery man riding it went head over tail. Wonton soup, roast pork, fried rice, and orange beef spilled onto the pavement. It took a few moments for Gulliver to recover. By the time he had, there was a crowd forming around him and the delivery man. Wobbly, Gulliver stood up. He looked to see if the man he had been following was anywhere in sight. No luck. He was gone.

Gulliver was disappointed and still stunned. He sank back down to the ground. The air smelled of garlic, ginger, soy sauce and hot mustard. He could not get the image of the man out of his head. He kept trying to place him. It was no good. The man had stayed beyond Gulliver's reach during the chase. He stayed out of the reach of Gulliver's memory as well. Then Gulliver's world grew dark.

CHAPTER ELEVEN

G ulliver couldn't quite make sense of it when he opened his eyes. He saw Rabbi, Ahmed and Nina standing over him. His head hurt a lot, and he was groggy. But he wasn't totally out of it. He took a second to take in where he was—a hospital room. Even if he had not heard the whir and ping of the machines, he would have known where he was. Hospitals had a one-of-a-kind smell. It was a cocktail of pine cleaners, alcohol and other chemicals he couldn't name.

Gulliver asked, "What hospital is this?"

"Wilton General," Rabbi answered.

"You had an accident," Nina said, pulling a chair up to his bed.

"Yeah, with a Chinese-food delivery man. How is he?"

Nina smiled that smile at him. The smile that tore at his heart. "They treated him for some cuts and released him."

Rabbi asked, "What happened?"

As Gulliver answered, he kept a careful eye on Nina. "I was following a man after my van blew up."

"What'd he look like?" Ahmed wanted to know.

"White, forty maybe, about six feet tall, two hundred pounds. Light brown hair going gray. He wasn't in the best of shape."

There was panic in Nina's eyes. She fought very hard not to let it show. She sat perfectly still and steady. Gulliver knew there was something she wasn't telling him. He just couldn't figure out what it could be.

"You think he was the guy that lit up your van?" Ahmed asked.

"Maybe. It didn't blow up all by itself. My guess is, he shoved a gas-soaked rag in the fill hole and put a match to it. I saw that guy through the smoke. He took off running when he spotted me."

"About the van," Rabbi said. "It's a total loss. There's a Wilton cop outside to talk to you about it. What are you going to tell him?"

"Forget that!" Nina barked at them. She took Gulliver's hand in hers. "Let Gullie be for now."

"No," he said. "It's fine. I'd rather get this over with. Rabbi, you'd better stay here as my lawyer."

"Whatever you want."

Now the panic in Nina was spreading. Her hand was shaking.

Gulliver winked at her. He said, "Don't worry, Nina. I won't mention Anka to the cop."

His words didn't make Nina's hand stop shaking. But he didn't press her about it.

The officer entered the room soon after Ahmed and Nina had left. He was maybe fifty. He had a big belly and a sneer on his face. Gulliver knew his type. The type of cop who resented Keisha for being a woman and for being black. He had probably retired at low rank from the NYPD. But he couldn't stay away from the job. So he'd joined a small police department. In Wilton, he could be a big fish in a very small pond.

"I'm Sergeant O'Toole of the Wilton Police, Mr. Dowd. Who is this gentleman?" The cop nodded at Rabbi.

Gulliver said, "Steven Mandel, attorney-at-law...*my* attorney-at-law."

That made O'Toole curious. "A lawyer. Do you feel you need a lawyer, Mr. Dowd?"

"He also happens to be my best friend, Sergeant. In any case, he's here and I want him to stay."

"That's your choice," said a displeased O'Toole. "When you were brought to this hospital, you had a 9mm SIG Sauer on you."

"And the permit to carry it," Gulliver was quick to say. "I'm a licensed PI."

"Yeah," the sergeant said, "I noticed that too. So what are you investigating in Wilton?"

"Who says I'm investigating anything? I stopped to have a cup of coffee on Main Street."

O'Toole didn't believe a word of it. "And you just happened to meet up with a blind kid dressed in a Bloomfield Prep uniform?"

"I was alone in the coffee shop. When the kid walked in, I asked him if he'd like to sit with me. My looks put some people off. With the kid being blind and all, I figured he was safe. We were having a pleasant breakfast when we heard a boom."

"That was your van exploding, Mr. Dowd. Correct?"

"Too bad, but yes. It was my van."

"Do you know who might've wanted to blow up your van or do you harm?" O'Toole asked.

Gulliver went on the offensive. "Do you think someone did it on purpose? Do you have any evidence that it was arson?"

"Well, no. We're still combing over the scene. But vans don't just go blowing themselves up," said the cop.

"I don't know anything about that, Sergeant. All I know is that I have to go through my insurance and have another custom-built van made for me."

O'Toole didn't quit. "All right, then maybe you can explain why you didn't stay with your van or call the police. You wound up several blocks away, where you got hit by the delivery guy."

"There wasn't anything I could do about my van. What can I say? I'm a sucker for the smell of good Chinese food."

O'Toole looked very unhappy. But Gulliver was in a hospital bed. He had his lawyer at his bedside. There really wasn't much the sergeant could do. "Are you kidding me with that answer or what?" he asked.

Gulliver knew it was time to stop. "I'm tired, Sergeant O'Toole. If you wouldn't mind, I think I'm done answering questions for now."

O'Toole was a stubborn bastard. He looked about ready to ask another question anyway. But Rabbi shook his head and said, "You heard my client, Sergeant. He's cooperated with you. Now, unless you have proof there was an act of arson or that my client committed a crime, please leave."

"Have it your way. But when your client gets out of here, I expect his first stop to be at the police station. We need to take his statement about today's events. Got it?"

"Loud and clear," Rabbi announced.

O'Toole didn't bother with goodbyes. He just turned and left. The sneer on his face was bigger now.

When Rabbi was sure the cop was gone, he spoke. "Gullie, who's Anka, and what the hell are you really doing here?"

"Rabbi, are you asking me as my friend or as my lawyer?"

"Both."

"My answer to my friend is that I cannot tell you," Gulliver said. "The answers are private and between me and my client. My answer to my lawyer is that Anka is Nina's daughter. She's gone missing. I'm investigating her disappearance."

Gulliver ached to tell Rabbi the whole truth. He wanted to say that he was Anka's father. Something deep inside him told him not to. He had told Vespucci only because he had to. Before he told anyone else, he had to find her. He had to meet her and talk it over with her. Then he could tell Rabbi. After that, maybe the rest of the world.

Rabbi was shocked. "Nina has a kid? Amazing. I never figured her as the kind of woman who wanted kids."

"Yeah," Gulliver said. "Pretty surprised myself. I've had a few surprises of my own recently. Now do me a favor and get a doctor so I can get the hell out of here."

CHAPTER TWELVE

Gulliver knew he shouldn't do it. But he knew he had to. So when the doctor released him from the hospital, he accepted Nina's offer to take him home with her.

He knew it was playing with fire. It was more than playing with fire. It was sticking his hand into a furnace. But it was a risk worth taking. Gulliver needed to know why she was so frightened. He also needed to know what she was holding back.

Nina's apartment was in Chelsea. It was just north of where Black and Blue Steaks was located. She had amazing views of the Hudson River, New Jersey and Lower Manhattan. The apartment was beautiful. The furnishings were works of art. They were one of a kind. Everything in the place was just so. From carpet to ceiling it was perfect. Nina always had had a taste for expensive and pretty things.

They hadn't talked much in the car on the ride down from Wilton. Gulliver didn't know Nina's reason for being quiet. He only knew his own. He had a crippling headache. The kind that made dying seem like a good option. It also made crawling into Nina's bed to sleep it off seem like a wise thing to do. He needed to fall down the well of sleep. He didn't care where the well was or how deep.

He opened his eyes. His headache was gone. Nina wasn't. She was asleep next to him. There was a dim light in the room. It was bright enough to let him see that Nina was naked. His heart raced at the sight of her. The warmth of her body next to his made him half-crazy.

As fumbling and awkward as their lovemaking had been back in high school, Gulliver had enjoyed every second of it. He had loved the afterglow of it even more. He would stay awake long after she had drifted off and watch her sleep. It was as if he couldn't believe how lucky he was. He'd wanted to be like a sponge. He'd wanted to soak in every second of their time together. Here they were again, older and wounded. But it was no less exciting for Gulliver. He watched her for a while. Then he quietly got out of bed to make his way to the bathroom.

Nina was awake when he got back.

"I thought you were trying to sneak away," she whispered.

"Nature called."

"How do you feel?"

"Much better."

She swung her bare legs over the side of the bed. "Come here, Gullie."

He hesitated. Not for long. He realized it was silly to fight it. He had wanted this for too long to let anything get in the way. He stepped toward her. Nina leaned forward and covered Gulliver's lips with her own. They kissed for what felt like forever. For Gulliver, it wasn't nearly long enough. Gulliver didn't stop her when Nina began to undress him.

Two hours went by like a snap. Nina was asleep again. Gulliver lay next to her, watching her. At some point he also gave in to sleep. But his was a restless sleep. His mind was busy putting together puzzle pieces from half-forgotten dreams. He dreamed of the flaming van and the man he had chased. He thought he almost had a name to put to the man's face. He never quite got it. Gulliver's mind wouldn't stay in one place. It jumped to the talk he'd had with Nina in the restaurant. Pictures of Colorado flashed in his mind. Joey Vespucci's words rang in his ears. Finally, he relaxed into sleep.

The next time he opened his eyes, the light in the room came from the morning sun. Nina was not alongside him. The bedroom still smelled of her. He called out to her. She did not answer. She must have gone out, Gulliver thought. He didn't worry about it. He just lay there, remembering the magic of how they had been together seventeen years ago. He thought about the magic of last night. Things had been much less awkward than in high school. The afterglow was no less warm. He hadn't felt so much like a whole person in a very long time. Gulliver had told himself he'd come here to question Nina. To find out why she was so scared. To find out what she wasn't telling him. Yet, in his heart, he knew he had gotten what he'd really come for.

In the shower, Gulliver happily let the water pour over him. He needed to find Anka more than ever. Maybe they could be a real family. He had been afraid to hope for it. After last night, he couldn't stop himself from hoping. Then it hit him in the gut like a cannonball. It took his breath away. All the hope he'd been feeling washed down the drain with the soap and water.

Gulliver called Ahmed and asked him to pick him up around the corner. He didn't wait in the apartment. He didn't want to see Nina yet. He threw on his clothes and got out of there as fast as he could. His clothes still stank. They smelled of the smoke from the van fire. They smelled of sweat. None of that mattered now. He thought he had the key to finding Anka. But he needed to get back to his place to do a little research.

CHAPTER THIRTEEN

G ulliver Dowd was not a big fan of
prayer. It was hard to pray to a God
who had played such cruel tricks on him
and Keisha. Still, he had prayed hard that
he was wrong now. But he wasn't wrong.
He had pretty much known that from the
moment the idea hit him in the shower.
At least God was consistent. This was His
cruelest trick of all.

The Internet could be an ugly place. But
it was also a PI's best friend. It hadn't taken
Gulliver more than ten minutes to track

down Nina's aunt in Colorado. And she was very willing to talk to Gulliver. She said Nina had spoken of him often while staying with her all those years ago. Gulliver had interviewed many people in his years as a PI. He knew that most people loved to talk if you just let them. Gulliver acted as if he was looking for Nina.

"I haven't seen her in many years," he lied. "We didn't end on a good note. I want to get past that."

The aunt chatted on. Gulliver mostly just listened to her talk.

"I hear Nina had a baby girl," he said.

"Anka's her name. Cutest baby ever." The aunt was full of pride. "She comes out here every summer to visit me. I'm more like her grandmother than a great-aunt. Her birthday's coming up next month."

"Really?"

"November first. I never miss it. I call her and send a card with some money."

"One of our old friends I talked to said Anka was born prematurely," Gulliver lied again. He knew that once you started lying, it got easier.

The aunt laughed. "Oh no, Mr. Dowd. Your friend got that all wrong. The baby was weeks late. They were about to induce Nina when she went into labor. Funny thing is, she barely even showed until the last month. Young girls are like that sometimes."

"Oh, I see. Is it true that Nina is a lawyer?"

There were a few seconds of silence. Then she said, "I'm afraid not. She owns a fancy restaurant back in New York. She was doing real well in school. Then the baby came. She also had a full-time job. Nina just couldn't keep up. She went back east a little over a year after she came out here."

"But not to her family on Long Island?"

"No," the aunt said. "My sister would have taken her back in a second. But my brother-in-law was a real ass. He shut out her and the baby. To this day they don't have anything to do with her."

Gulliver backtracked. "You said Anka comes to visit you every summer."

"Yeah, every summer."

"Pardon me for being nosy. But your voice changed when you said that. Did something happen? Was she sick or something?"

"Nothing like that," the aunt said quickly. "No, some man kept pestering her."

"Did you go to the police?"

"I wanted to. Anka made me promise not to. I let it go. But I did tell Nina about it. A mother has a right to know these things."

They talked a little more. Gulliver stayed away from touchy subjects. He didn't want to make the aunt wary.

"Please do me a favor," Gulliver said before hanging up. "Please don't tell Nina I called. When I get in touch with her, I want it to be a big surprise."

The aunt liked that idea. "You have my word. Nina could use some old friends. I didn't much care for the friends she made after she left here."

Gulliver's next call was to Joey Vespucci. One of those friends Nina had made after she left Colorado.

"Hey, little man," Vespucci said when he picked up the phone. A smile was in his voice. "How you doing?"

"Good, Joey."

"You know what? Nina ain't called me yet to thank me for letting her off the hook."

"That's because I haven't told her yet. I wanted to get this thing with her daughter wrapped up first."

Joey was curious. "You know where the girl is?"

"Not exactly. I have a pretty good idea of who she's with and how to find her."

"Is there going to be any trouble? You need some extra muscle?" Joey offered.

"No thanks. I don't think it'll be any trouble at all," Gulliver said. "There is one thing that I wanted to ask you, Joey."

"Shoot."

"Was Nina a hooker when you met her?"

"You didn't ask Nina?"

"The time didn't seem right," Gulliver answered. "Was she a hooker?"

"Not exactly. She was an escort. Very high-class girl."

"So what you're telling me, Joey, is that she was a high-priced hooker."

"That's about it. Let's just say I acquired the business. And I saw that Nina had other talents. She was made for better things. I taught her the business. She ran my clubs for me for many years. I guess I always had kind of a soft spot for her. That's why I made the deal to lend her the cash for the steakhouse. In return, all she had to do was front the clubs."

"Are you okay talking about this on the telephone?" Gulliver asked.

"Don't worry," Joey said. "The line is safe. Thanks for asking. Most people would be too selfish to ask."

"Just one more question. Was Nina ever arrested when she worked for you, or when she worked as an escort?"

"A couple of times. Nothing serious. My lawyers always got her out of it."

Gulliver was numb when he hung up the phone. He was sick that Nina had played him for a fool. But mostly he hated her for the *way* she played him.

But he'd taken the job. And he never quit on a job. Never.

CHAPTER FOURTEEN

The next day the air around the coffee shop in Wilton still smelled a little like burnt van. Gulliver thought maybe the smell was in his head. Ahmed said no. He smelled it too. At least the van had been towed away. Gulliver wasn't there about the van. He was there to take the next-to-last step in finding Anka. He and Ahmed had already stopped at the Wilton Academy to talk to Henry. Henry was the security guard who'd seen the older man and Anka at the coffee shop in town. It had cost Gulliver another hundred dollars.

It was money well spent. Gulliver had asked Henry if he could remember the date he'd seen them. He'd answered immediately.

"Absolutely. September eighteenth. It's my mom's birthday. I'd just ordered her flowers from the shop down the street," he said.

Gulliver had one more question. "Did you see cash on Anka's table when you came into the coffee shop?"

"That's a weird question, Mr. Dowd."

Gulliver handed the security guard another twenty-dollar bill. "Humor me. Try to remember."

Henry squeezed his eyes shut. He whispered to himself loudly enough for Gulliver and Ahmed to hear. "I walked into the coffee shop and said hello to Judy the waitress. I turned to my left. I noticed the girl sitting at the only dirty table in the place. She was holding a gift-wrapped box. There was a shopping bag on the floor next to her.

A seat was pushed back from the table. There were dirty dishes on the table in front of the girl and..." Henry opened his eyes and said, "No. There was no cash on the table. I hope that helps you."

That had been a half hour ago. Now Ahmed and Gulliver walked into the coffee shop. A lone woman in her fifties stood behind the counter. It was the woman who'd served Gulliver the day before.

"Judy?" Gulliver asked.

"That's me," she said. "Oh, you were in yesterday with the blind kid. Wasn't it your van—"

Gulliver nodded. "Yes. That was my van." He showed her his PI license and a photo of Anka. He explained that the girl was missing.

"Sweet girl. Good tipper. In here all the time."

"With the blind kid and sometimes with an older man?"

Dirty Work

Judy was surprised. "That's right! How did you know that?"

Gulliver winked at her. "I'm a PI, remember? It's my job to know."

"But how can I help?" Judy asked.

"Do you still have your credit-card receipts from September eighteenth?"

"Sure do," she said. "Wait right here."

Once they had the credit-card receipt, the rest was simple enough. Gulliver knew how to put a trace on a card. It didn't take more than five minutes for the credit-card company to call him back with a hit.

* * *

The Pink Flamingo Motel wasn't pink. And it wasn't much of a motel. But it was cheap, and it wasn't very far from Wilton. The desk clerks at places like the Pink Flamingo didn't care much about their guests' privacy. It only took twenty bucks

and one look at Ahmed to get the clerk
to give them the room numbers. Gulliver
had Ahmed call Nina to ask her to come
over to the motel. It would take her more
time to get there than Gulliver needed.

Ahmed parked the Escalade far
enough away from the rooms not to be
spotted. He got out of the Caddy and
peeked in some windows.

"They're both in his room," Ahmed
told Gulliver when he got back.

"Okay. I'll walk over. You pull the
Escalade up in case they run. But they
won't run. I'll handle this."

Gulliver climbed down out of the suv.
He took the second-longest walk of his life.
The longest was when he went to iden-
tify Keisha's body. It had nearly killed him
to see his sister that way. This walk was
almost as hard. He knew what he would
find today. And it would crush the joy
right out of him. The sweet hope he had

felt only a few hours ago was gone. But Gulliver knew he couldn't turn away from the truth. He would not run from it.

He knocked on the door. Gulliver saw Ahmed pull the Escalade forward. Then the hotel room door opened. In the doorway was the man Gulliver had chased the day before. The man's name no longer escaped him. He knew who he was. It had been a long time since Gulliver had seen him this close up.

"Hello, Gulliver," said the man. "Anka and I have been waiting for you."

"Hello, Eddie. Has it really been seventeen years?"

Eddie Gorman laughed a sad laugh. "It was yesterday."

"It *was* yesterday." Gulliver laughed too. His laugh was sadder than Eddie's. "I mean, before yesterday. It was seventeen years."

"Something like that."

Gulliver stepped into the room.
Seated at a desk was Anka Morton. She
was even more beautiful in person. On
a chain around her neck was a piece of
jewelry. It was a Sachem North High
School ring. He would bet that was the
only thing missing from the jewelry box
in her dorm room. Anka smiled a huge
smile at Gulliver.

"My god, you're Gulliver Dowd!" Her
voice was something like her mother's.
"My mom used to talk about you all
the time."

"Gulliver," Eddie said, "this is—"

"Your daughter, Anka." Gulliver
finished the sentence. "Nice to meet you,
Anka." He bowed to her.

Gulliver had known the truth since
the puzzle pieces came together for
him in Nina's shower. He'd been pretty
sure after talking to Nina's aunt. Joey
Vespucci had gotten rid of any doubts.

Eddie and Anka were father and daughter. There was no denying it. With some people, you just know they're related. Eddie Gorman had dated Nina all through high school. He had given Nina the ring Anka now wore on a chain around her neck. Then Eddie and Nina broke up, in the spring term of their senior year. It didn't take a rocket scientist to figure out the rest.

"My mom lied to me for my whole life, Mr. Dowd," Anka said. "She always told me she never knew who my father was."

"That's between the three of you to talk over. But I'm working for your mom. She's on her way up here right now. You should sit down together and work it out. Right here. Right now. That's my advice."

"But my mom lied to me. It's the worst kind of lie."

"People lie, Anka. That's what they do. They lie for all sorts of reasons. They lie to hurt each other. They lie to get what they want. They lie because they're afraid. Sometimes it's because they think lies will protect the people they love. Talk to your mom. You may hate her now. But she's the only mom you're ever going to have."

Gulliver couldn't take being with Anka anymore. He excused himself, saying how lovely it had been to meet her. Eddie followed him out of the room. "I know Nina. She told you Anka was your daughter."

"She sure did. She knew it would get me to find her."

"I'm sorry, Gulliver. I really am. She's a great kid."

"I would have been proud to be her dad. You treat her right, Eddie. You treat her like a father should or I'll come for you."

"Don't be mad at me. It's Nina who did all the lying here."

"Sorry," Gulliver said. "You're right."

"I'm sorry about the van. It was a stupid stunt. I just panicked. I wanted to scare you off. I thought it would take longer for the van to blow. I thought I would have more time to get away. I've been looking for Anka for so long. I didn't want to lose her. Not now."

"I get it."

Eddie went on. "I don't have much money. It will take some time for me to pay you for the van."

Gulliver offered up his right hand to Eddie. "Forget it. My insurance will pay for it."

They were shaking hands when Nina pulled into the lot.

CHAPTER FIFTEEN

A week had passed since the day at the motel. Gulliver had told Rabbi and Ahmed about Nina's lies. That Nina had known all along that Eddie Gorman was Anka's father. That she knew he had come for her. The worst part was that Nina had known she was pregnant when she started dating Gulliver in high school. Nina had used Gulliver's good heart to trick him into doing her dirty work now. Rabbi was sick with anger. Ahmed took it in stride. Ahmed's calmness bothered Gulliver.

"Know what your problem is, little man?" Ahmed didn't wait for Gulliver to answer. "Problem is, you don't pay no mind to what your own eyes see. All your life, people treat you all wrong. But you keep thinking someday things will change. Like, that someday one good thing will happen and the world won't be like it has always been. I see the world for what it is. So it doesn't shock me when someone pulls some bad stuff like Nina did."

There wasn't much Gulliver could say. Ahmed was right. Gulliver believed in hope in spite of himself. He believed in hope in spite of his bitter life. He believed in hope in spite of all the hurt. He hoped things could change. He had to. Without hope, life would not be worth living. Like when he was praying to God, even though in his heart he knew Anka wasn't his. He guessed his parents' goodness had rubbed off on him more than he thought.

None of that mattered now. Nina was sitting in front of him. She was in the same chair she had sat in when she'd told him Anka was his daughter. He'd thought about never speaking to her again. He'd thought about shutting her out of his life. But he knew he had to see her one last time. He needed to cut her out of his life. He could not run away like he had the last time. He had to say it to her face. He could not let his anger be like an open wound. He did not want to let that wound bleed him dry one drop of bad blood at a time.

"Say your piece, Nina. Please do me a favor. Don't say you are sorry. It would be one more of your lies. And I wouldn't believe it."

"Okay, Gullie. The truth?"

"That would be a nice change."

"I deserved that," she said. "I knew Eddie got me pregnant. I couldn't tell him. He would have wanted to marry me.

I wasn't ready for that. There was no way I was going to get married so young. I also could not marry a guy whose big goal in life was to sell insurance for his dad."

Gulliver sneered. "You had bigger dreams."

"You bet I did. They didn't include marrying an insurance salesman," she said.

"No, not you. Your big dreams involved fucking strange men for money."

"Don't stop there, Gullie. Sometimes women, too. Sometimes women and men together. It was business. I fucked you, didn't I? I knew once I slept with you, I could sleep with anyone. It's a good lesson to learn if you are going to sell yourself for money. Those two months in high school taught me I could do anything I needed to."

She'd said it. He'd known it was coming. But knowing it was coming didn't make it hurt less. It felt like she had stuck a dull knife into his stomach and twisted it. He even winced a little.

Gulliver smiled in spite of his hurt. "You're right. I guess if you could sleep with the likes of me, you could do just about anything. But I am still a little confused."

"About what?" she asked.

"Did you care about me at all?"

Now *she* looked hurt. "I loved you. But mostly I felt sorry for you. It also gave me cover in case Eddie ever got the idea the baby was his. I did what I had to do. I always have. Anka is no worse for it."

"Don't be so sure," he said.

"What's that supposed to mean?"

"Nothing, Nina. Parents rub off on their kids no matter what. A month from now, Anka will be the same age you were when you got pregnant."

"You bastard," she hissed. "You little bastard. To think I really loved you once. The problem with you is that you still believe in that kind of love. We were stupid kids. What did you think was going to happen if we stayed together? Did you think we were going to ride off into the sunset? Wake up, Gullie. I wasn't going to marry an insurance salesman. I wasn't about to marry you either. Go read *Romeo and Juliet*. The only way that kind of love lasts is if the couple dies young."

"You're right, Nina. You came out of this way ahead. You used me to get Anka back. Well, you got her back. And guess what? You got a bonus. Joey Vespucci's letting you off the hook. Have your lawyer call his lawyer. You've got your restaurant free and clear. I guess you got everything you wanted."

"I did, didn't I?" she said. "Thanks for doing me that favor with Joey. Him letting me off the hook is an added bonus. I got Anka back. Eddie says he only wants to see her a few times a year. All these years I was afraid he'd take her from me. That's not going to happen now."

Gulliver shook his head. "You're right again. He's not going to take her. You've already driven her away. Your lies will haunt you, Nina. Eddie seems like a good man. He won't have to take her. Anka will turn to him. Eddie's smart. He knows that. He can give her the one thing you never gave her. The truth. You betrayed her. You betrayed Eddie. You betrayed me. People are pretty forgiving about most things. Not betrayal."

"What is that supposed to mean?"

"You know exactly what it means," he said. "I wouldn't pay Anka's tuition too far in advance. She will walk out of school the minute she turns eighteen. She will run as far away from you as fast as she can, into Eddie's arms. And you won't be able to do a damn thing about it." Gulliver was done. He hopped down off his chair.

Nina had a sour look on her face. It made it hard to see her beauty. "Where are you going?"

"As far away from you as fast as I can get there. Goodbye, Nina."

That was that. Gulliver Dowd left Black and Blue. His heart was pounding as he walked through the door. His heart had felt this way only once before. It was on the day he buried Keisha. This time he was burying seventeen years of hopes and dreams. He was done doing Nina's dirty work forever. Gulliver hailed a cab on Little West 12th Street. He didn't look back.

ACKNOWLEDGMENTS

Thanks to Bob Tyrrell and David Hale Smith. Also to Sara J. Henry for her editorial advice and keen eye. As always, thanks to Rosanne, Kaitlin and Dylan. Without them, none of this would matter.

* * *

Called a "hard-boiled poet" by NPR's Maureen Corrigan and "the noir poet laureate" in *The Huffington Post*, Reed Farrel Coleman has published fifteen novels. He is a three-time recipient of the Shamus Award for Best PI Novel of the Year and a two-time Edgar Award nominee. He is an adjunct professor of English at Hofstra University and lives with his family on Long Island. For more information, visit www.reedcoleman.com.